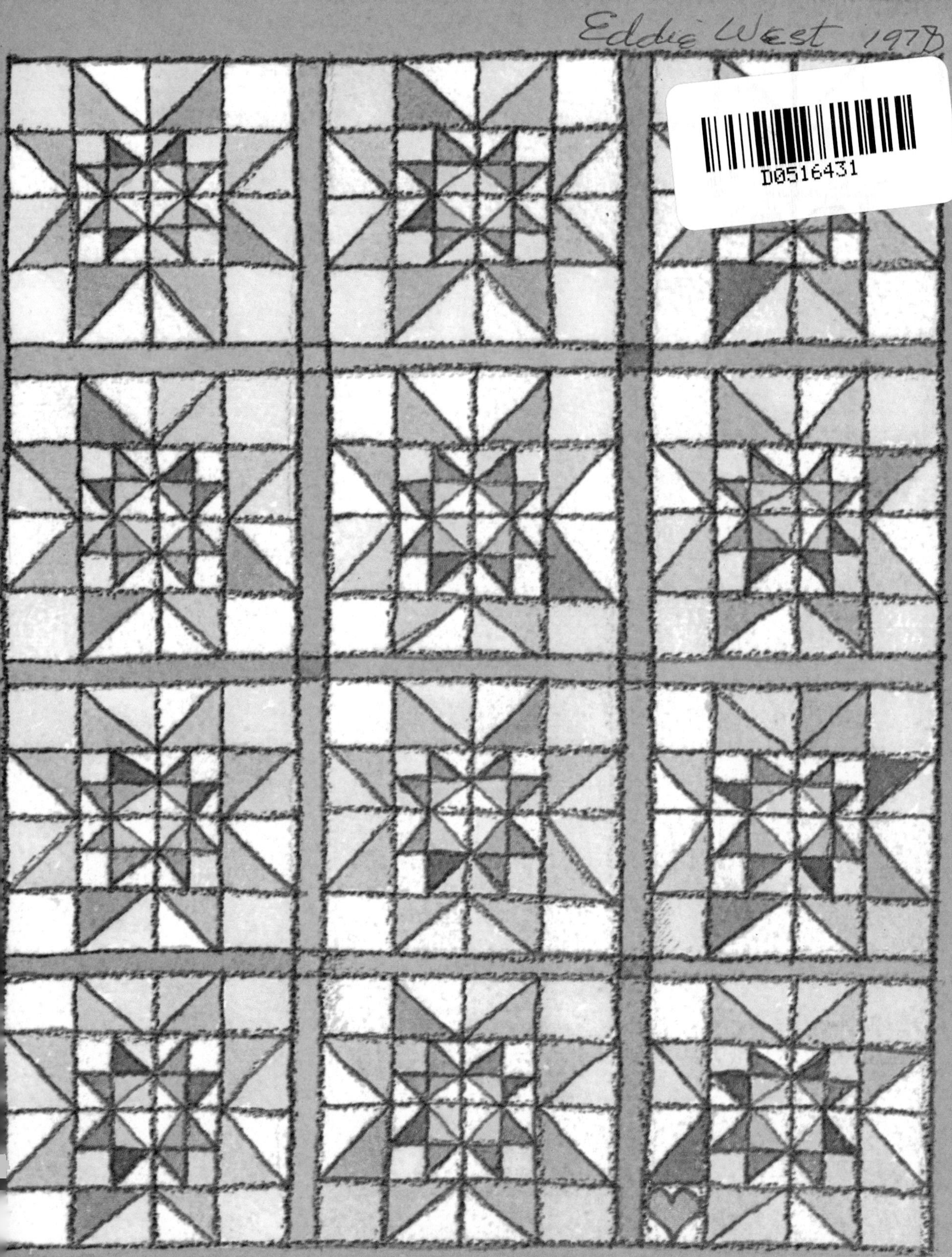
Eddie West 1978

# OLD MAN WHICKUTT'S DONKEY

*Story by*
Mary Calhoun

*Pictures by*
Tomie de Paola

Parents' Magazine Press / New York

*To Jodi, who keeps on smiling*

One day Old Man Whickutt set off down the mountain with his donkey and his boy, going to the mill. Donkey, he carried a sack of corn; boy, he carried a stick; and Old Man Whickutt, he carried the boss words to keep them both going straight.

"Heeyuh, donkey! You keep moving! Wake up, boy! Poke the critter with your stick!"

So the donkey kept moving, and the boy kept poking, and Old Man Whickutt kept talking, so's they'd need him along.

Well, that was an edgy sack of corn on the donkey's back. It slid over to one side, and the donkey walked all skeewonkus to balance it. Sack slid down by his ears, so the donkey rared back.

Then it slid toward his tail, so he kicked up
his heels.

"Derned fool donkey!" said Old Man Whickutt.
"Acts as addled as a hen with its head off.
Here, we'll sling the sack under his belly.
That's the way to carry a sack."
"Haw-w-w!" said the donkey.

They tied the sack onto the donkey's underside, and the donkey, he walked all spraddle-legged to keep from kicking it as they went on down the road.

Pretty soon they came along by Granny Pollard's cabin, Granny herself a-rocking on the porch.

"Hi there, Whickutt!" she called out. "How d'ye do?"
"Plumb wore out already, and still a far way to go."
"Then how's come you're walking when you got a
donkey to ride?" asked Granny.

"You're right! Sure's the jaybird nested on the **fence!**" said Whickutt. "Why didn't I think of that?"

Old Man Whickutt got onto the empty spot on the donkey's back. "Get along, donkey!" says he.
"Huhhhh!" says the donkey, dawdling.
The donkey was so small and the old man's legs so long that his feet slid along on the ground.
Sack of corn, it slumped on the ground, too, so they unslung the sack, and the boy carried it.

"Shove the critter with your stick," said Old Man Whickutt. "I could walk faster'n this."
Fact, he did walk his feet a little to help the donkey along.

"Why did the jaybird nest on the fence?" the boy wanted to know. He'd never heard of a bird so foolish.

The old man set in to telling, but he hardly had
it rightly explained before they met
Preacher Hawkins, a-striding up the trail.

"Shame on you, Whickutt!" said the preacher.
"Taking your ease on that donkey, while your poor
little boy has to walk and carry a load, too.
You oughta let the lad ride."

"You're right, sir," said Whickutt. "Sure's an angel has got two wings! Here, boy, you get up."

So the boy climbed onto the donkey's back, and
the old man walked, carrying the sack. And
the boy tickled the donkey's ears with his stick,
and the donkey said, "Heeee!" and they all
went on down the road.

But before long they came to Mother Jones,
a-hanging her wash in the sideyard.
"Well, I declare! What a lazy boy!" called out
Mother Jones. "And what a foolish grandaddy,
to let his boy ride, while he walks and carries
the load, too!"

"Well, I'll be a one-eyed woodpecker's uncle!"
exclaimed Old Man Whickutt. "You're derned if you do,
derned if you don't! All right then,
shove up there, boy."

So the boy shoved up front on the donkey's back, and the old man climbed on behind, hefting the sack. The donkey squalled, "Eee-huhhh!" and they all went on down the road. The donkey, he was kind of sagging.

But then they came to the Perkins family,
a-picking berries beside the trail, and they all
bust out crying, "Oh law! Look at that!
Poor little donkey! Why, you'll break the beast's
back with such a heavy load! Might as well
pile on the church and the belltower, too!"

"I couldn't please the devil himself today,"
growled Old Man Whickutt. "Derned if you don't,
derned if you do!"

Still, he kept trying. Just then the donkey collapsed, a-snorting and a-blowing, legs splayed out on the ground. So the old man took pity on the poor little critter.

"Donkey's turn to ride!" declared Old Man Whickutt.

First he tied the sack of corn on the donkey's back, next he hoisted the donkey's front legs on the boy's back, and then he picked up the donkey's hind legs. And Old Man Whickutt and the boy carried the donkey all spraddled out.

"Eeee-hawww!" sighed the donkey.

Along came a wagonload of folks, and everybody pointed, laughing fit to split.

"Well, the bear's found the berry bush!" cried
Old Man Whickutt. "Pleased somebody at last!"

So they went on that way until they came to the
creek. And they hadn't ever crossed that creek
before, at least not the donkey and the boy and
Old Man Whickutt all together.
Creek water was flowing pretty high, too.
"Hmmm. Gonna get that sack of corn wet,"
mumbled Old Man Whickutt,
"sure's lightning follows thunder."

The miller stood over on the other side of the
creek, and he looked long and hard at that sight
of a donkey riding in such style.
"Hey there!" he called out. "What you oughta do is—"
"Never mind what I oughta do!" Whickutt shouted
back. "I'm derned if I do, derned if I don't!
And derned few snakes can straddle a stump,
so I'll please myself."

Then Old Man Whickutt took and threw the sack of corn over the creek to the other side. Then he took and threw the boy over the creek. Then he took and threw the donkey over the creek.

And then, by gum, Old Man Whickutt, he took and threw himself over the creek to the other side.

So nobody got wet.

Derned if they did!